Why the Sky Is F

A Nigerian Pourquo

retold by Antonio Blane
illustrated by Gerardo Suzán and A Corazón Abierto

Long ago, the sky was close to the ground. People could touch the clouds. They could touch the moon.

Best of all, the sky was made of food. People could take a piece of sky any time. They could eat at any time. Some people said the sky tasted like corn. Others said the sky was as sweet as a yam.

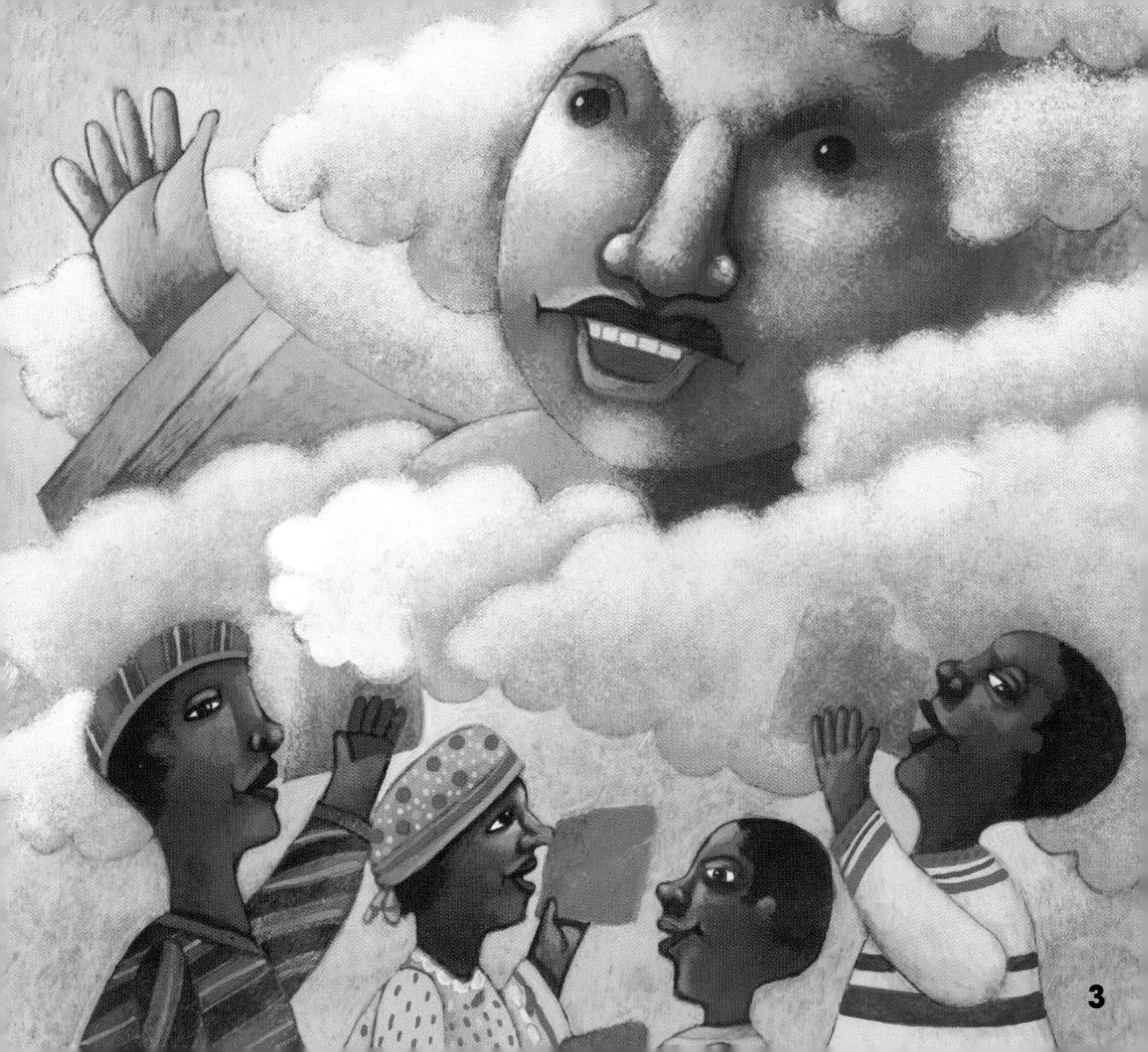

People did not need to farm. They did not need to hunt or fish. People spent their time painting, singing, and playing games.

Most people were happy to share the sky, but a few people were greedy. They took big pieces of the sky and ate just a little. Then they threw away the rest.

Sky grew sad. "People are wasting my gifts," he cried. "King, come to me!"

The king of the people raced to the sky. "Oh kind and mighty Sky, what is the problem?" he asked.

Sky said, "I have been good to the people. I have asked for only one thing in return: Do not waste the sky or there will not be enough to feed all the people."

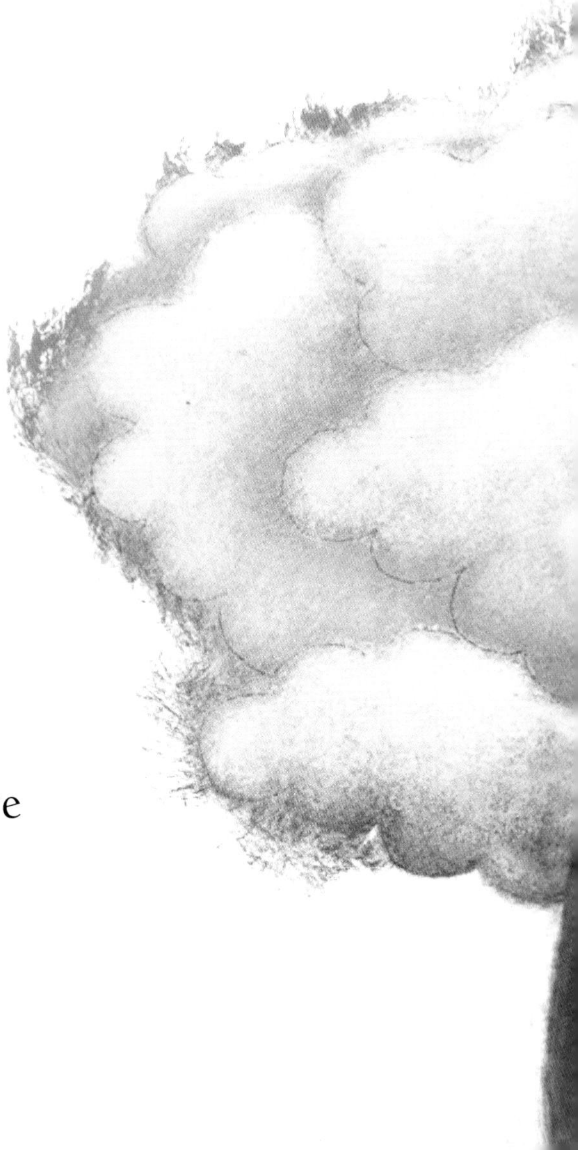

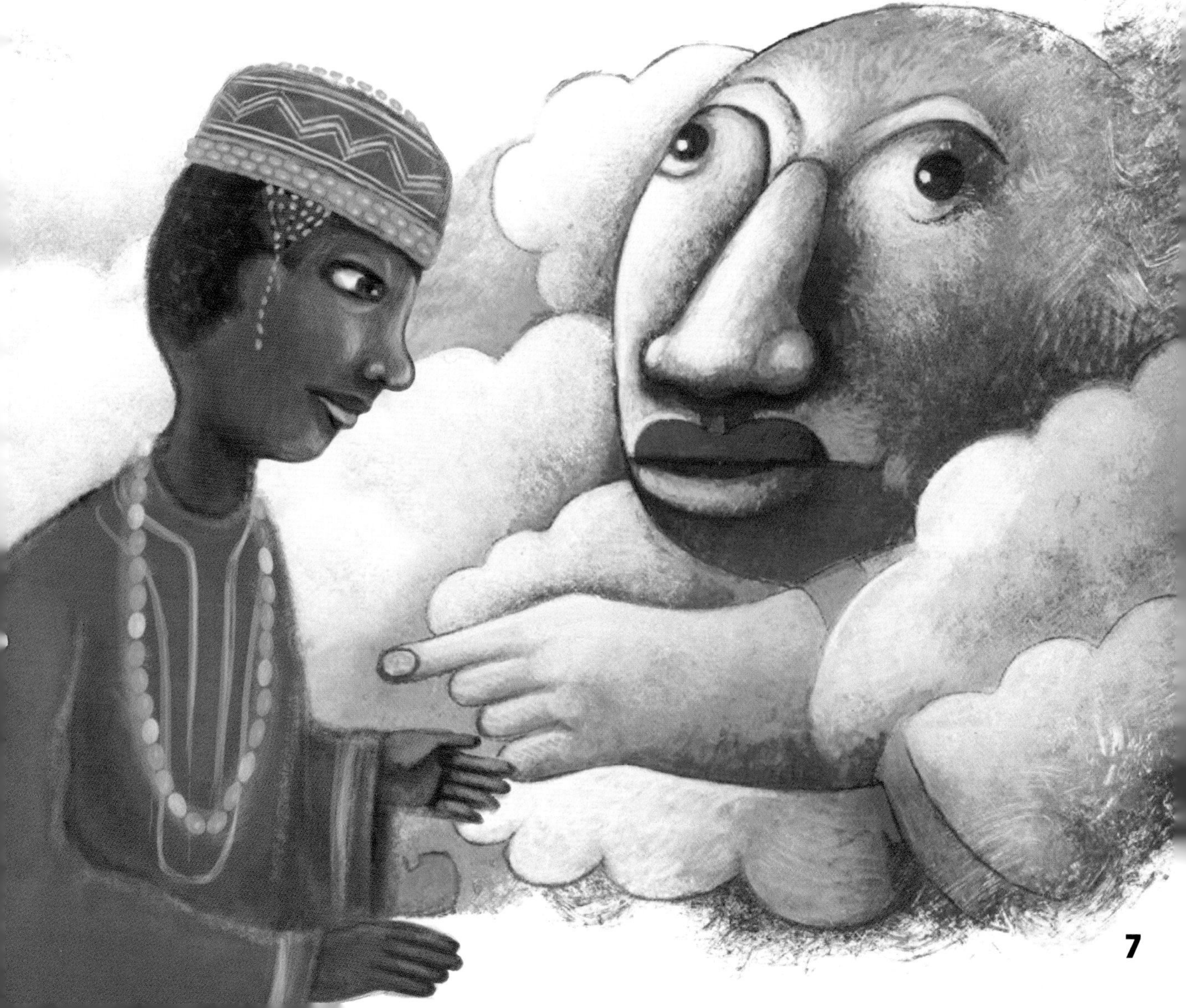

"I have told the people to be careful," said the king. "Most have listened. But some people have not. I will tell them again." The king bowed.

"Thank you," said Sky.

The king called his people together. "Never take more sky than you can eat. The sky is a gift. If you waste it, the sky will fly away," he said. "We have one more chance."

Most people said they would be more careful, but one group did not. They did not listen to anyone. "Let the others be like sheep," said this group. "We will do what we want."

That night, the greedy people took one
mile of the sky. They ate just a tiny
bit and buried the rest behind their
home. They did not think they
would be found out.

But Sky saw what the group did. Sky got angry. His voice boomed like thunder. "You have not listened, people. I will now leave this world. I will take the sun. I will take the moon. I will take the clouds with me into space," he said.

"Please don't leave us,"
the king begged Sky.

13

Sky was mad. But he also felt bad. He knew
that many good people were on Earth.

Sky reconsidered his decision and announced, "I will let the sun, moon, and clouds stay near. But I must go far away. From now on, people must learn to plant. They must hunt for food. They must learn to fish."

15

So the sky floated up to where it is today.
And that is why the sky is far away.

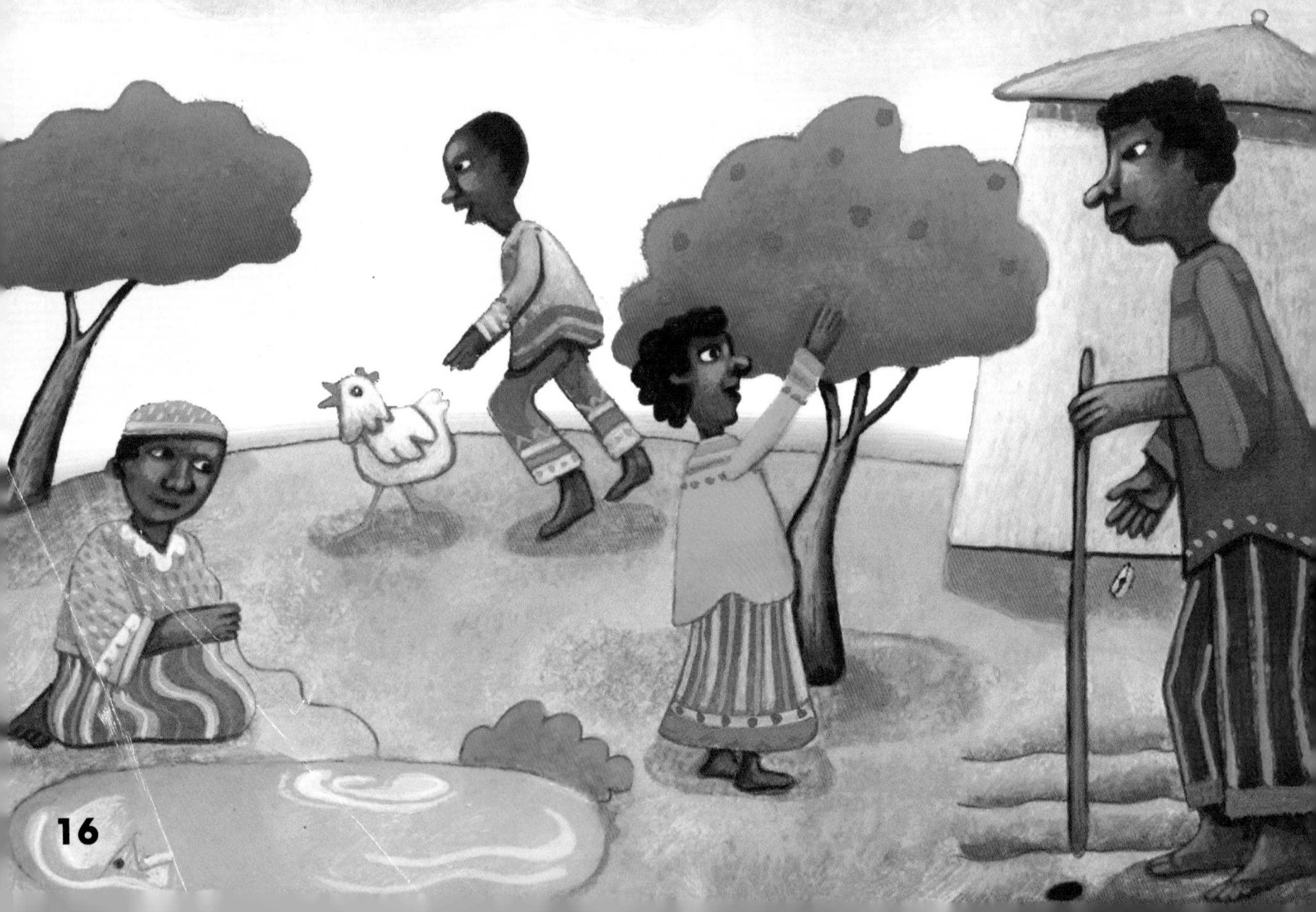